GREAT ILLUSTRATED CLASSICS

PETER PAN

J. M. Barrie

adapted by
Marian Leighton

Illustrations by
Allen Davis

BARONET BOOKS, New York, New York

GREAT ILLUSTRATED CLASSICS

edited by
Joshua E. Hanft

Contents

About the Author

Sir James Matthew Barrie was born in Scotland in 1860. His father was a weaver. His mother, who had a very strong personality, was the dominant figure in his life.

Barrie studied at the University of Edinburgh. He began his career as a journalist, writing for various newspapers and magazines. In 1885 he moved to London and began to write novels. His early works drew from his experience of Scottish life.

The publication in 1891 of *The Little Minister* established Barrie's reputation as a novelist, and its performance on the London stage in 1897 led to his recognition as a playwright.

Barrie's best known creative work by far was *Peter Pan*. It was first produced in the

London theater on December 27, 1904 and was an instant success. The book appeared in 1911 under the title *Peter and Wendy* (later called *Peter Pan and Wendy*).

Although Barrie became famous for *Peter Pan*, his most skillfully written play was *Dear Brutus*, which was written in 1917. It contained elements of both tragedy and comedy. It also resembled *Peter Pan* in its blend of reality and make-believe.

Barrie became an English baron in 1913 and was appointed to the Order of Merit in 1922. From 1930 until his death in 1937, he served as chancellor of the University of Edinburgh.

Barrie's marriage was unsuccessful—a fact that some observers laid to his failure to mature emotionally. Perhaps, like Peter Pan, the author never wanted to grow up!

The Darlings

Chapter 1

The Darling Family of England

Their last name was Darling, and it suited them perfectly. The father, George, met and fell in love with his wife when both were very young. They had a fairy-tale wedding: Mrs. Darling was a beautiful bride in a long white dress, and Mr. Darling was a handsome groom. They had three children: Wendy, John, and Michael. The parents were very devoted to their daughter and sons, but Mr. Darling worried constantly about the family budget and the cost of such basic items as milk.

All of the families in their London neighborhood hired nurses for their children. The Darlings, who didn't have much money, "hired" a special kind of nurse: a large dog called Nana! She performed her duties quite as well as any human nanny. She bathed and dressed the children, tended to them if they woke crying in the night, and walked alongside them to school, keeping them safe when they crossed streets. She even carried an umbrella in her mouth so that they would stay dry in case of rain.

When Nana tucked Wendy, John, and Michael into bed, she always left the night light on, because the children were frightened of the approaching Neverland. Each child had a different picture of this place and the things that happened there, and in fact it didn't seem scary. It was just that the children had an uneasy feeling of losing control of their surroundings and drifting off to that dream world

She Even Carried an Umbrella.

where anything might happen.

Since all three children belonged to the same family, their dreams of the Neverland were a lot alike. Peter Pan appeared in all of them but seemed especially real to Wendy. Even Mrs. Darling, thinking back to her childhood, could remember a character called Peter Pan, who was believed to live in fairyland.

"Surely Peter Pan is all grown up by now," Mrs. Darling joked with her daughter.

"No, mommy, he will never grow up. In fact, he is just about my size!" Wendy replied.

Her father pooh-poohed the whole idea of Peter Pan.

"Nana probably put the whole idea into the children's heads," he told his wife. "Dogs have such ideas! Don't worry about Wendy. She'll forget about Peter Pan soon enough!"

But Peter Pan would not let them forget him. In fact, he appeared at the Darlings' house that very night!

That Very Night!

"Look! He forgot to wipe his feet, and there are leaves on the floor," Wendy remarked to her mother the next morning.

"Who are you talking about?" Mrs. Darling asked.

"Peter Pan, of course!"

"But how could he get into the house without knocking?" asked her mother, trying to play along with Wendy. "The door is always locked."

"He came in through the window! You can see that the leaves are next to the window!"

Mrs. Darling could not bring herself to tell Wendy that it was all a dream. After her daughter went downstairs for breakfast, she even examined some of the leaves. They didn't look at all like the ones that grew on the trees next to the house!

"He Forgot to Wipe His Feet."

She Too Fell Asleep.

Chapter 2

Peter Arrives

An unbelievable event was about to shatter the peaceful life of the Darling family, but there was no hint of it as Mrs. Darling helped her children get ready for bed one night.

It was Nana's night off. The mother gave the children their baths and sang them to sleep. As she sat sewing in the nursery, she too fell asleep.

She dreamt that the Neverland came too close and that a strange boy broke through its curtain and approached Wendy, John, and

Michael.

And, in fact, while she was dreaming, a boy did enter the room through the open window! He dropped swiftly to the floor. Dressed in a suit of leaves, he carried a small light as he flitted about the nursery. The light awakened Mrs. Darling. She gasped, knowing at once that it was Peter Pan!

When she regained her breath, Mrs. Darling screamed in fright. Nana had just returned from her evening out and came bounding through the door. She sprang at the boy, but he flew quickly out the window and disappeared into the night in the form of a shooting star.

Nana closed the window too late to capture Peter, but she caught his shadow. The dog hung the shadow out the window, figuring that Peter could come back and pick it up without coming into the house and bothering the children.

The next morning, Mrs. Darling decided

Dressed in a Suit of Leaves

that hanging a shadow outside the house would ruin the look of the whole neighborhood. She rolled it up and placed it carefully in a drawer. There it stayed until the following Friday.

"If only I hadn't accepted the invitation to dinner at Number 27," Mrs. Darling moaned afterward whenever she remembered that dreadful Friday evening.

"If only I hadn't poured my medicine into Nana's bowl!" cried Mr. Darling.

The evening had both started and ended badly. First, Michael refused to take a bath and kept climbing off Nana's back when she tried to carry him to the tub. Then Mr. Darling, who hated to get dressed up in party clothes, couldn't knot his tie.

Next, Nana brushed against Mr. Darling, covering his new suit with dog hairs. Finally, there was the problem with Michael's medicine. Nana held it on a spoon in her mouth, but

She Rolled It Up Carefully.

Michael refused to take it.

"Be brave, Michael! Be a man!" his father said. "When I was your age, I always took my medicine!"

"How about taking it now?" suggested John. "I mean that medicine that you sometimes take."

"But it tastes disgusting!" protested Mr. Darling.

"It can't be as bad as mine!" chirped Michael.

"It's worse!" answered his father.

"I have an idea!" said Wendy. "Why don't you both take your medicines?" Before Mr. Darling could object, she ran into the bathroom and returned with the bottle and a spoon.

"Now both of you take it at the same time!" she ordered.

Michael swallowed his medicine obediently, but Mr. Darling slipped his behind his back.

"Father!" scolded all three children.

"It's Worse!"

Feeling ashamed, Mr. Darling tried to turn their attention away.

"I'll tell you what!" he said. "I'll put some medicine into Nana's bowl, and she'll think it's milk."

Mrs. Darling and the dog came into the room.

"Come here, Nana!" said Mr. Darling, "and drink this milk." The children stared him in anger but did not dare to criticize him.

Nana lapped up the "milk" from the bowl, then let out a painful cry and crept to her kennel. The children sobbed.

"Stop feeling sorry for that dog!" Mr. Darling shouted at them. "I've had quite enough of her trying to be the boss of this family! I won't let her stay in the nursery one more night!" He seized the dog, dragged her outside to the yard, and tied her to a tree. Then he sank into a chair, not daring to face the children after performing this wicked deed.

"Drink This Milk."

Mrs. Darling tucked the children into their beds, lit their night lights, and prepared to leave the room. Outside, they could hear Nana barking.

"She's *so* unhappy," said John.

"That's not her unhappy bark," Wendy corrected him. "That's the way she barks when she smells danger!"

Mrs. Darling went nervously to the window. It was securely fastened, but she remained fearful.

"If only I didn't have to go to a dinner party tonight!" she thought to herself.

The children sensed her fear.

"Can anything harm us when the night lights are lit?" asked Michael.

"No, sweetheart," she answered. "They are the eyes that a mother leaves behind to guard her children when she goes to bed."

Michael flung his little arms around her neck. "I love you!" he murmured. Those were

"She Smells Danger!"

the last words that she would hear from any of the children for a terribly long time.

Mr. and Mrs. Darling walked to the party at Number 27. The stars watched from above. They knew that Peter Pan was planning something important and was waiting for the grown-ups to get out of the way. How he hated grown-ups!

"Let the fun begin, Peter!" whispered the smallest star as the elder Darlings entered Number 27.

Mr. and Mrs. Darling Walked to the Party.

Thousand Times Brighter than Night Lights

Chapter 3

An Invitation to the Neverland

Alas! The three night lights blinked and went out almost as soon as the children fell asleep. But now there was another light in the nursery. It was a thousand times brighter than the night lights, and it moved swiftly around the room in search of Peter Pan's shadow. It shone into all the drawers, the closets, the shelves, and into the pockets of all the children's clothes.

The light belonged to Tinker Bell, a fairy that was no larger than a person's hand. She was dressed in a costume of leaves that was full and square and sparkled with silver fairy dust.

A moment after the fairy entered the nursery, little stars blew the window open and Peter dropped in. He checked the three beds to make sure the children were asleep. Then he called softly to Tinker Bell, "Do you know where they put my shadow?"

She pointed to the chest of drawers. Peter opened it and grabbed one item of clothing after another, tossing everything onto the floor. Soon he found his shadow.

Peter Pan had never been separated from his shadow before, and he imagined that it would simply attach itself to him. When it didn't, Peter flew angrily into the bathroom and tried to stick it on with some soap, but he failed. Now Peter was frightened. He sat down on the floor next to Wendy's bed and began to cry.

Peter Dropped In.

His sobs awakened Wendy, who sat up in bed.

"Boy, why are you crying?" she asked, not feeling a bit scared at the sight of the stranger in the room.

Without answering, he arose and bowed politely to her.

"What is your name?"

"Wendy Moira Angela Darling. What's yours?"

"Peter Pan."

"I knew it! I knew you'd be Peter Pan! But is that your whole name?" she asked.

"Yes," he replied, thinking for the first time how short it was.

"I'm so sorry," said Wendy Moira Angela.

"It doesn't matter," Peter gulped.

"Well, where do you live?"

"Second to the right," replied Peter, "and then straight on till morning."

"What a funny address!"

"Why Are You Crying?"

"No, it isn't!" he snapped.

Wendy apologized, remembering that Peter was a guest in her house.

"But is that the address that people put on letters?"

"I don't get any mail," said Peter.

"But your mother must get letters," Wendy persisted.

"I don't have a mother."

He didn't tell her that he was glad about that. He thought grown-ups were very over-rated. But Wendy, feeling a great surge of pity for him, ran to his side.

"No wonder you're crying!" she exclaimed.

"I'm not crying about mothers. I'm crying because I can't get my shadow to stick back on," he said.

Then Wendy saw the shadow on the floor. She tried not to laugh when she realized that Peter had tried to make it stick with soap.

"I know exactly how to help you," she said.

"I Don't Have a Mother."

"I will sew it on. It may hurt a little bit, but try not to cry any more."

"What do you mean to 'sew'?" asked Peter.

Without replying, she took a needle and thread and attached the shadow to Peter's foot.

"Maybe I should also iron it," she suggested. "It's very creased."

"What do you mean to 'iron'?" asked the boy.

"Never mind," she said, knowing that boys didn't care how their clothes looked.

Suddenly Peter, already forgetting Wendy's great help, pranced around and shouted: "How clever I am! I've put my shadow back on!"

Wendy, angry, forgot about being the good hostess. She jumped back into bed and covered her head with the blankets.

"Don't go away, Wendy Moira Angela!" he pleaded. "I just can't help being pleased with myself."

When she still refused to come out, he tried

She Attached the Shadow to Peter's Foot.

flattery.

"Wendy, you know that one girl is more useful than twenty boys!"

Wendy could resist neither his voice nor his praise. She peered out from the covers and, a few minutes later, moved to sit beside him on the bed.

"What you said is very nice," she began. "Now I'd like to give you a kiss, if you don't mind."

Peter, not knowing what a kiss was, held out his hand. Wendy moved her face toward Peter, but he simply dropped an acorn button into her hand.

She moved her face away and said that she would be pleased to wear his kiss on the chain around her neck. Little did she know that wearing that button on the chain would save her life one day!

"Now that we've been introduced," she said, changing the subject, "tell me how old you are,

"One Girl Is More Useful than Twenty Boys!"

Peter."

Peter squirmed and looked uncomfortable.

"I don't know," he finally replied, "but I am very young."

This boy was certainly full of mystery! Wendy thought.

"I ran away from home the day I was born," Peter continued. "It was because I heard my father and mother talking about what I should become when I grew up. You see, Wendy, I don't ever want to be a grown-up. I want to be a little boy always and to have fun. So I ran away to Kensington Gardens to live with the fairies."

Wendy stared at him with fascination. She had always stayed very close to home and never had a chance to meet any fairies. Peter, feeling sorry for her, told her all about them.

"There ought to be one fairy for each boy and girl in the world," he concluded. But lots of children no longer believe in fairies. Every

"I Ran Away the Day I Was Born."

time a child says 'I don't believe in fairies,' a
fairy somewhere falls down dead. Speaking of
fairies, I wonder what happened to Tinker
Bell."

Wendy clutched Peter's hand.

"Do you mean there's a fairy in this very
room?"

"She was just here. Listen!"

"The only sound I hear is like bells tinkling,"
said Wendy.

"That's Tink!" exclaimed Peter, "and that's
fairy language! But it's coming from the drawer. I do believe that I shut Tinker Bell in the
drawer when I grabbed my shadow!"

He opened the drawer, and the fairy flew
out, talking rapidly to Peter. Wendy couldn't
understand a word of the conversation, but she
could tell that Tinker Bell was angry.

"Don't worry about her," said Peter to
Wendy. "I told her she could be your fairy, because you're both girls, but she still wants to

The Fairy Flew Out.

be *my* fairy."

Wendy and Peter were sitting in the armchair now, and she kept bombarding him with questions.

"Where do you live most of the time?" she asked.

"With the lost boys," Peter said.

"Who are they?"

"They're the children who fell out of their baby carriages when the nurses weren't paying attention. If they weren't claimed by their families in seven days, they were sent far away to the Neverland. I'm their captain!"

"Oh, that must be lots of fun!"

"Yes," said Peter, always plotting his next move, "but we're sort of lonely. There are no girls to keep us company. Girls are much too clever to fall out of their baby carriages!"

"I think it's perfectly lovely the way you talk about girls," said Wendy. "I *do* wish to give you a kiss."

"Where Do You Live?"

She leaned toward him and planted a kiss on his face. Then she let out an awful scream.

"What happened, Wendy?"

"It felt like someone was pulling my hair!"

"It must've been Tink. She is really naughty sometimes! And she says she'll do that to you every time that you kiss me!"

Peter stood up and walked toward the window.

"Don't go!" Wendy cried out. "I will miss you!"

Peter stayed a while longer, but Wendy was disappointed when he told her that he came to the nursery window not to see her but to listen to the stories that her mother told her before bedtime.

"I don't know any stories," he said. "The lost boys don't either."

"Stay, Peter! I know lots of stories."

"Well, then come and tell them to the boys!" he declared, drawing her toward the window.

A Kiss on His Face

"You know I can't go with you!" she protested—although she was pleased that he had invited her. "What about my parents? And, anyway, I can't fly!"

"I'll teach you!"

"Oh!" she murmured.

Peter, sensing that he could persuade her, pressed on.

"I'll show you how to jump on the wind's back and fly around and talk to the stars."

"Oh, really?"

"And you'll meet the mermaids!"

"Oh, how I'd love to see a mermaid!" Wendy was so excited she felt that she could hardly keep her feet on the floor.

"You could tuck us in at night!" Peter continued. "None of us has ever been tucked in at bedtime. And you could sew our clothes and even make pockets. None of us has any pockets!"

Knowing that she could no longer resist this

"How to Jump on the Wind's Back"

adventure, Wendy asked, "Peter, would you teach John and Michael to fly too?"

Peter wasn't that interested in the boys, but he agreed, and their sister quickly woke them up. Then they all grew silent, the way children do when they hear sounds from the grown-up world. Nana, who had been barking unhappily all evening, had suddenly stopped.

"Hide! Quick!" said John. "Someone is coming!"

Liza, the cook, entered the nursery holding Nana on a leash. Liza was in a very bad mood because the dog's constant barking had disturbed her work in the kitchen. She had finally decided to bring the animal to the nursery to see for herself that the children were all right. But Nana, standing in the doorway of the dark and silent room, was still suspicious. She tried to spring away from Liza, but the woman would not let go. She took the dog back to the yard and chained her to the tree again.

"Someone Is Coming!"

After Liza returned to the kitchen, Nana made a mighty effort to get free of her chain. At last, she broke it. She raced full speed to Number 27 and burst into the dining room where Mr. and Mrs. Darling were seated. Sensing immediately that something was terribly wrong, they followed Nana back home without even saying goodbye to their hostess.

She Raced Full Speed.

Peter Wasted No Time.

Chapter 4

Flying Away

Peter Pan, meanwhile, wasted no time. He flew around the nursery, to the delight of the children. Then he urged each of them to try. It was no use.

"Maybe we'll have to stay home after all," sighed Wendy, thinking it was probably for the best. But Peter continued to coax her.

"You'll miss the mermaids!" he declared. Turning to John, he said, "There are also pirates!"

"Pirates! Let's go at once!"

They all tried again to fly. But it was not possible, until Peter sprayed fairy dust on them. He blew a small amount on each child. The results were amazing! As Mr. and Mrs. Darling and Nana hurried home, they looked up and saw shadows on the curtain of the locked nursery window of three little figures in night clothes circling in the air!

No! There were *four* figures!

They would have reached the nursery in time if the stars, watching them closely, hadn't blown open the window and whispered: "Hurry, Peter!"

Peter Pan knew there wasn't a second to spare. "Come!" he ordered the children. He flew out into the night, followed closely by Wendy, John, and Michael. Moments later, the children's parents and dog rushed into an empty nursery. Outside the window, the stars seemed to be laughing.

These stars guided Peter Pan back toward

Fairy Dust

the Neverland with his new friends. The group was flying "second to the right, and straight on till morning," as Peter had described it. This was the way to Neverland, but Wendy wondered how Peter Pan could find it without getting lost. There were so many seas and hills and buildings!

At first, the children were so excited by the adventure of flying that they didn't worry about what might happen to them. They lost all track of time as night became day and day turned back into night. They frequently bumped into clouds. But the most frightening thing was when they grew tired and began to fall out of the sky. Peter would wait until one of the children was about to crash into the ground or the ocean before he would rescue them. He was more concerned with showing off than with saving their lives.

"I'm hungry!" John complained.

"Don't worry," said Peter, approaching a bird

Second Star to the Right

and snatching some food from its beak. The bird grabbed it back, and a mile-long chase followed. This became the method of capturing a bite to eat during the flight.

Peter was not only a show-off, but he could be mean as well.

"There goes Michael!" he said once as the littlest child suddenly fell asleep and dropped toward the earth.

"Save him! Save him!" screamed Wendy. But Peter simply smiled at her distress and waited an unbearably long time before catching her brother. Nevertheless, Wendy understood that they must be nice to Peter.

"Think what would happen if he abandoned us," she told John and Michael.

"We could go back," said Michael.

"How would we ever find our way back home without Peter?"

"Well, then, we could go on," declared John. "We would *have* to go on, because Peter never

"Save Him! Save Him!" Screamed Wendy.

taught us how to stop!"

"I guess that if we kept going, we would eventually reach home, because the world is round," offered Wendy. But she didn't want to take any chances.

Peter, who could fly so much better and faster than the rest of them, often disappeared from view for what seemed like hours. He would come back and describe a conversation with a star or a mermaid. But what if a time came when he didn't return to them?

"There it is!" exclaimed Peter after a long period of silent flight. "Look! All the arrows are pointing!"

Indeed, a million golden arrows, splashed with sunlight, pointed out the island of Neverland. The place seemed familiar to the children from past dreams, but now it was no longer make-believe. After the arrows disappeared, Neverland looked dark and gloomy and there were no night lights and no Mommy,

A Million Golden Arrows

Daddy and Nana to wake up to.

The children and Peter flew closer together now. They were flying so low that they touched the tops of the trees. Everyone sensed danger.

"They don't want us to land," Peter declared. But he wouldn't explain who *they* were.

"Do you want to have an adventure right now or just stop for tea?" he asked. Wendy wanted tea, but John wasn't sure.

"What kind of adventure?" he asked.

"There's a pirate asleep in the field just beneath us. If you like, we'll go down and kill him," said Peter matter-of-factly.

"What if he wakes up?" asked John.

"I never kill pirates while they're sleeping!" replied Peter in a tone of anger. "I always wake them up before I kill them!"

"Oh my! Do you kill many?"

"Oh, yes! And there are more pirates on the island now than ever before!"

"Who is their captain?" asked John solemnly.

Flying So Low They Touched the Trees

"Hook. Captain James Hook."

A fearful look came into John's eyes, Wendy shuddered, and Michael began to cry. They had all heard of the vicious Hook.

"Is he very big?" John asked, looking in awe at Peter.

"Not as big as he was before. I cut off a bit of him."

"May I ask what bit?" asked John, with great admiration in his voice.

"His right hand."

"Then how does he fight?"

"He has an iron hook where his hand used to be, and he claws with it!"

Peter looked sternly at John. "You must make the promise that every boy who serves under me makes. That is, if we meet Hook in battle, you must leave him to me!"

"I promise," said John loyally.

Tink, who had flown on ahead, now rejoined them. She brought the news that the pirates

They Had All Heard of Hook.

had sighted them and had gotten out Long Tom, their biggest gun.

"They spotted us because of Tink's light," Peter told the children.

"Tell her to put the light out!" they cried in fear.

"She can't do that," Peter explained. "The light goes out by itself when she falls asleep, just like the stars."

"Well, then, we must keep the light hidden," said Wendy.

"Let's put Tink in John's hat," Peter suggested. The fairy agreed to travel in the hat, but she became annoyed when John handed the hat to Wendy.

They flew on in silence. Suddenly a shot from Long Tom pierced the stillness. No one was hurt, but the force of the shot carried Peter far out to sea. Wendy was blown upwards and found herself alone with Tinker Bell. She would have been better off if she had

"Let's Put Tink in John's Hat."

dropped the hat and flown alone.

Tink hated Wendy because she was jealous of her. Now she plotted to destroy the girl. She jumped out of the hat and motioned to Wendy to follow her. Confused and frightened, Wendy plunged toward her doom.

Tink Was Jealous of Wendy.

Circling Around the Island

Chapter 5

A Make–Believe Place Come True

Neverland began to throb with life as its inhabitants sensed that Peter was returning. The lost boys went out to look for Peter, the pirates went to look for the lost boys, the Indians went to look for the pirates, and the beasts went to look for the Indians. Since each group was circling around the island at the same speed, they didn't find each other.

The boys, wearing the skins of bears that they had killed, were walking in single file. Each held a dagger. The number of boys on the island varied. Some grew up, which was against Peter's rules, and some left. Tonight there were six, counting the twins as two.

Tootles was the gentlest and the most humble of all the boys. He also had the worst luck. It seemed that every time he left the group—even for a few minutes—an adventure would happen and he would miss it. He would return to find the other boys cleaning up from their latest victim.

Nibs was known for his cheerful nature, Slightly for his snobbishness and Curly for his habit of taking the blame for wrong-doing whether or not he was really at fault. Finally, there were the twins, who always stayed close together.

The pirates were walking rapidly around the island, singing their dreadful song:

"Avast belay, yo ho, heave to,
A–pirating we go,

Tonight There Were Six.

And if we're parted by a shot,
We're sure to meet below!"

Never was there a more vicious and wicked-looking band. The pirate Cecco was known for writing his name in letters of blood on the bodies of his victims. Bill Jukes, who once killed six dozen men in a single day, was covered with tattoes. Gentleman Starkey loved to kill as much as the rest of the band but was very dainty in his methods.

The ship-mate Smee maimed people just for the fun of it. He named his weapon Johnny Corkscrew because it looked like a corkscrew that people use to remove corks from wine bottles.

Other members of the pirates' band worth mentioning were Noodler, whose hands were attached backwards, and Skylights.

The fearsome Captain James Hook lay comfortably in a chariot borne by his men. He was the largest and darkest of the group. His long

Never a More Wicked-Looking Band

hair was arranged in curls that looked like black candles. His blue eyes didn't seem to fit with the rest of him, but during his evil acts they gleamed horribly and red spots appeared in them.

Captain Hook had a reputation for amazing courage; but he was said to cringe at the sight of his own blood, which was thick and had an odd color. A contraption that enabled him to smoke two cigars at the same time dangled from his mouth.

By far the grimmest thing about Captain Hook was the iron claw that had replaced his right hand. Hook's method of operation was always the same: He would choose a victim, tear him with the claw, and then kick the body aside, all the while continuing to puff on the two cigars.

Such was the terrifying enemy of Peter Pan. Which of the two would win the ultimate contest for control of Neverland?

The Grimmest Thing about Captain Hook

The Indians who lived on the island were noted for their cruelty. They moved noiselessly around the island, constantly on the trail of the pirates. They carried tomahawks and knives, and their bodies gleamed with warpaint and oil. The scalps of pirates hung on ropes around their necks.

The first Indian in line was always Great Big Little Panther. He carried so many scalps that it was hard for him to walk. Bringing up the rear was Tiger Lily, an extraordinarily brave and beautiful young woman who held the male members of the tribe at bay with her hatchet.

On this night of Peter's return, the Indians were heavy with food and drink, but the beasts who followed them around the island were lean, mean, and hungry. The beasts included lions, tigers, bears, and other man-eaters. Their tongues were hanging out as they searched for prey.

Bringing Up the Rear Was Tiger Lily.

A gigantic crocodile was among the beasts. This creature was searching for a particular target. The reader will soon discover his identity.

After the boys had circled the island many times, they stopped to rest near their home.

"I wish Peter would hurry back," said Tootles. "I want to hear about Cinderella and all the other stories that he knows. I'm sure that my mother was just like Cinderella."

The others nodded. They were not allowed to talk about mothers when Peter was there, but now they conversed freely. A sound in the distance soon forced them into silence, however. It grew steadily closer. It was the pirates, singing their hideous song:

"Yo ho, yo ho, the pirate life,
The flag o' skull and bones,
A merry hour, a hempen rope,
And hey for Davy Jones!"

In a moment the boys, scampering as quick-

A Crocodile Among the Beasts

ly as rabbits, disappeared into their home.

Home was a most unusual place! The pirates had tried to find it for a long time, but the entrance was invisible. In fact, there were seven entrances. Only by moving aside piles of brushwood could a visitor discover them. They were holes hollowed out of tree trunks, and each hole was the size of a boy.

As the pirates moved forward, Starkey glimpsed Nibs disappearing through the forest. He aimed his gun, but Hook's iron claw stopped him.

"Let me kill him!" Starkey pleaded.

"No!" declared Hook. "The noise of the shot will bring Tiger Lily's Indians upon us! Do you want to lose your scalp? Anyway, one isn't enough; I want *all* of those boys!"

Hook turned to Smee, his most loyal follower.

"Most of all, I want their captain, Peter Pan!" he confided. "He cut off my arm and

Nibs Disappearing Through the Forest

flung it to a crocodile that was passing by."

"No wonder you are so frightened of crocodiles!" Smee remarked.

"Not all crocodiles," Hook corrected him. "Just that one crocodile. It liked my arm so much that it has followed me ever since, licking its lips for the rest of me!"

Hook sat down on a large mushroom and stretched out his claw.

"That crocodile would have gotten me already, Smee, but it swallowed a clock that keeps ticking. Whenever I hear the tick, I run to get away."

"Someday," replied Smee, "the clock will stop working, and then the crocodile will get you."

"That's the fear that haunts me," Hook admitted. Then suddenly he winced in pain.

"What's the matter?" asked Smee.

"This seat is hot!" Hook exclaimed. "I'm burning up!"

He jumped up at once, and the two pirates

"It Liked My Arm So Much!"

examined the mushroom. It was the largest one they had ever seen. When they tried to pull it up, it came loose at once, because it had no root. Even more strange, smoke started to rise from the spot where the mushroom had been.

"A chimney!" cried Hook.

The pirates had indeed discovered the chimney of the lost boys' underground home. The boys stopped it up with a mushroom whenever enemies were in the neighborhood.

The boys were chattering loudly, talking about plans to welcome Peter Pan home. Listening from above to the conversation, the pirates grinned and put the mushroom back in its place. It was then that they noticed the holes in the seven trees.

"Time to put your plan into action, Captain!" laughed Smee, rubbing his hands in anticipation of capturing the boys.

"Right!" said Hook. "We'll return to the ship

"A Chimney!" Cried Hook.

and cook a big thick cake with green sugar on it. We'll leave the cake on the shore of the mermaids' lagoon. The boys always swim there and play with the mermaids. They'll find the cake and gobble it up. Before long, they'll die!"

"What a delicious plan!" exclaimed Smee. And they began to sing:

Avast, belay, when I appear,
By fear they're overtook,
Nought's left upon your bones
When you
Have shaken claws with Cook."

As they finished, another sound came to their ears: Tick tick tick tick.

"The crocodile!" gasped Hook. He bounded away, followed by Smee.

The boys emerged from underground, safe for a while longer.

"Look! A great white bird is flying this way!" Nibs shouted. All eyes turned toward the sky.

"It looks so weary, and it keeps moaning,

"The Crocodile!" Gasped Hook.

'Poor Wendy,' " observed Curly.

"Yes, there are birds called Wendys," recalled Tootles.

Wendy was now almost directly overhead. Behind her flew Tinker Bell. The jealous fairy was darting at the girl from every direction and pinching her savagely.

"Peter wants you to shoot the Wendy!" Tink called out to the boys.

"OK!" replied the boys in a single voice. They never questioned Peter's orders. They popped down their trees to fetch bows and arrows. Tootles was the first to return.

"Out of the way, Tink!" he shouted. In a moment, he had fired, and Wendy fluttered to the ground with an arrow in her chest.

"Shoot the Wendy!"

"It Must Be a Lady!"

Chapter 6

A New Mother

"I have shot the Wendy! Peter will be so pleased!" said Tootles with a smile. But the other boys did not smile back at him as they gathered around Wendy's body.

"This is not a bird!" cried Slightly in horror. "I think it must be a lady!"

"Peter must have brought her to us," said Nibs, "and now we have killed her!"

At this tragic moment, Peter landed. The boys stared him and quivered in fear.

"What kind of greeting is this?" he asked.

The boys were too frightened to speak.

"Well, never mind," laughed Peter. "I have some good news! I have brought you a mother!"

There was still no reply. Peter looked troubled.

"Haven't you seen her? She flew this way."

Finally, the boys pointed to Wendy's body on the ground. Peter just stared at first; then he gently removed the arrow from her chest and turned to the boys.

"Whose arrow is this?" he asked solemnly.

"Mine," said Tootles.

As Peter grabbed a bow and aimed the arrow at Tootles, Curly exclaimed:

"Look! The Wendy lady is moving her arm! She is alive!"

Peter knelt beside her. He saw that the arrow had hit the button on the chain around Wendy's neck. The button he gave her had saved her life!

Too Frightened to Speak

"Listen to Tinker Bell crying!" said Nibs, pointing to the fairy overhead.

"It was Tink who told us to kill the Wendy," Tootles told Peter.

The boys had never seen Peter look so angry.

"Go away!" he told the fairy. "And don't come back for a long time!"

What was to be done with Wendy while she recovered?

"Let's carry her down to the house," Slightly suggested.

"No!" replied Peter. "You mustn't touch the lady; that would be disrespectful."

"But if she just lies here, she will die!" said Tootles.

"Let's build a little house around her!" said Peter. He measured Wendy to try to decide how big the house should be. "Quick, boys! Bring all the tools and building materials you can find!"

Just then, John and Michael appeared.

"Tink Told Us to Kill Wendy."

They were so tired from flying that they could hardly stand up, but Peter made them work too.

"We are building a house for Wendy," he explained. "We are all her servants."

"But Wendy is only a girl!" John protested.

Suddenly Wendy began to sing:

"I wish I had a pretty house
The littlest ever seen,
With funny little red walls
And roof of mossy green."

The boys were delighted, because it just so happened that the branches they carried were red with sap, and the ground was covered with green moss. They sang back to Wendy:

"We've built the little walls and roof
And made a lovely door,
So tell us, mother Wendy,
What are you wanting more?"

She answered immediately:

"Oh, really next I think

"We Are Building a House."

I'll have
Gay windows all about,
With roses peeping in, you know,
And babies peeping out."

The young builders made windows by smashing their fists through the branches, and they used yellow leaves for curtains. But for the roses and the babies they had to use make-believe.

Now the house was finished, but they could no longer see Wendy, because she was inside.

"You must knock on the door and see if she will let you in," said Peter, "and be sure to be very polite and behave like gentlemen."

There was no knocker, so Tootles offered to make one with the sole of his shoe. Wendy answered the door. All the boys took off their hats.

"We've built this house for you," Nibs told her.

"It's lovely!" Wendy smiled.

Yellow Leaves for Curtains

All the boys knelt before her and held out their arms, pleading, "Oh, Wendy lady, please be our mother!"

"Do you really think I should?" she replied. "I'm only a little girl, and I don't have much experience."

"That's OK," Peter chimed in. "You're still a motherly person."

Wendy thought for a moment.

"Very well," she said. "I will do my best. Come inside at once, you naughty boys! Your feet must be cold and wet. And before I tuck you all in bed, I promise to tell you the story of Cinderella!"

"Please Be Our Mother!"

Peter Measured Them for Hollow Trees.

Chapter 7

The House Underground

When Wendy recovered fully from the arrow, she would spend her evenings with the boys in the underground house; then she would go to sleep in her own little house, with Peter standing guard outside against the pirates and beasts.

Peter measured Wendy, John, and Michael for hollow trees. Since no two people were exactly the same size, everyone had to be fitted for a tree in order to be able to go up and down quickly and easily.

They all loved their underground home. It consisted of one very large room. Mushrooms grew on the floor, and they were used as stools. A tree kept trying to grow in the center of the room, but every morning the boys sawed the trunk to make it level with the floor. By teatime, the tree was always tall enough to use for a table; after tea, it was sawed away to make more play space.

The room also had a fireplace. Wendy stretched a string above it to dry the washing. A huge bed stood along one wall of the room. All the boys, including John, slept in it. Since it was so crowded, no one was allowed to turn unless a signal was given, at which time everybody turned at once!

Michael slept in a basket, so that Wendy could pretend that he was her baby.

One section of the room belonged to Tinker Bell, and it was separated from the boys' area by a curtain. Tink had beautiful furniture and

Their Underground Home

clothes and was extremely neat.

Wendy tried to teach the boys to read and write. Most of them tried hard to learn, but Peter didn't have the time or patience for such things. He was the only boy in Neverland who couldn't write or spell the simplest word. Wendy would try to help herself and her brothers remember their parents by giving them test questions such as "What color was Mother's hair? How tall was Father? What did Nana look like?"

Wendy was so busy with her sewing, washing, and cooking that some days she never managed to get above-ground. The family ate roasted breadfruit, yams, coconuts, baked pig, mammae-apples, tappa rolls, and bananas and drank large amounts of poe-poe. Sometimes the meals were real and some were make-believe; it all depended on Peter's wish. But the make-believe meals were so real to him that you could see him getting fatter as he "ate."

To Read and Write

Adventures, like meals, were also sometimes real and sometimes make-believe. On some days, Peter went out alone, and when he came back you couldn't be sure whether he'd had an adventure or not. Sometimes he himself was unable to remember!

Wendy was absolutely certain about some of the adventures because she was part of them. Take the times that she found the cake that the pirates had baked to poison the boys. They put it in one clever spot after another, but on each occasion Wendy snatched it from the hands of her "children." Finally, it became as hard as a rock and no longer tempted the boys.

Wendy also witnessed an adventure in which Peter challenged the beasts by drawing a circle around himself on the ground with an arrow and daring them to cross it. Wendy and the boys watched breathlessly from the nearby trees, but hours passed and finally the beasts retreated into the forest.

Wendy Found the Poison Cake.

Mermaids Played in the Water.

Chapter 8

Danger in the Lagoon

The lagoon on Neverland was a pool of many brilliant colors. Mermaids played games in the water and, when they finished floating and swimming, they took sunbaths on Marooners' Rock. The rock got its name because evil ship captains often marooned sailors there, leaving them to drown when the tide rose over the rock.

Whenever the children appeared at the lagoon, the mermaids swam out of sight. The mermaids were very unfriendly toward Wendy and the boys, except for Peter. He often chatted with them on the rock, and one day he gave Wendy one of the combs that they used for their long hair.

Wendy made a rule that the boys must rest on the rock for half an hour every day after their mid-day meal—even if it was a make-believe meal. She sat beside them and did her sewing. The rock was not very large, but the boys were used to crowding together in their bed, so they weren't uncomfortable.

On the day of this adventure, a sudden change came over the lagoon. The sun disappeared, though it was still afternoon, and it became so dark that Wendy was hardly able to thread her needle. The water turned suddenly cold. In the distance, Wendy heard the sound of oars from a boat.

Wendy knew that she should awaken the sleeping boys, but she didn't want to break her rule about the half-hour nap after lunch.

He Often Chatted with Them.

Luckily, Peter sensed the danger even as he slept. He jumped up and held his hand to his ear.

"Pirates!" he shrieked. The children rose with a shudder.

"Dive!" Peter ordered. In an instant, the rock was empty.

The pirate ship approached. Smee and Starkey were aboard, along with Tiger Lily, who was their captive. They had caught her climbing onto the ship with a knife in her mouth. Now they hoisted her onto the rock, where she would be left to die.

Peter and Wendy were bobbing up and down in the water near the rock. Wendy felt great pity for the Indian girl, but Peter was angry because the pirates didn't fight fair—it was three to one against Tiger Lily.

Peter could have waited for the pirates to sail away before rescuing Tiger Lily, but he never chose the easy way to do anything. In-

"Pirates! Dive!" He Ordered.

stead, he imitated the voice of Hook:

"Ahoy, there, you lubbers!" he called.

"It's the captain, said Smee to Starkey. "He must be swimming out to meet us."

"We're marooning Tiger Lily," Smee called out.

"Set her free!" came the voice.

"*Free?*" cried Smee in amazement.

"Yes, cut her ropes and let her go!"

"But, Captain..."

"At once, d'you hear," the voice demanded, "or I'll plunge my hook into you!"

"This is strange," said Smee.

"Better do what the captain orders," said Starkey nervously.

"Ay, ay," Smee answered, and he cut the cords on Tiger Lily's feet. She slid rapidly into the water and disappeared.

Wendy greatly admired Peter's clever trick; but before she had time to praise him, the voice of the real Hook roared out over the lagoon:

"We're Marooning Tiger Lily."

"Boat ahoy!"

Smee and Starkey held out a lantern to guide Hook toward the ship. Peter and Wendy saw his iron claw grip the boat's side as he climbed aboard. He sat down on the deck and sighed deeply.

"What's wrong, Captain?" asked the men.

"The game's up," said Hook sadly. "Those boys have found a mother!"

"Oh, evil day!" cried Starkey.

"What's a mother?" asked Smee.

Suddenly they saw a strange sight. The Never bird's nest was floating on the lagoon, and she was sitting on it.

"There's a mother," said Hook to Smee. "The nest must have fallen into the water, but a mother never deserts her eggs."

Smee had another idea.

"If she's a mother, maybe she's hanging around here to help Peter."

"That's the fear that haunts me," Hook

"The Game's Up."

admitted.

"Captain!" said Smee eagerly. "Why don't we kidnap the boys' mother and make her *our* mother?"

"That's an excellent thought!" Hook replied. "We will seize the children and carry them to the boat. We'll make them walk the plank, and then Wendy will be our mother!"

They grinned broadly as they left the boat and climbed onto the rock. Suddenly Hook remembered Tiger Lily.

"Where is the Indian?" he demanded.

"Well, we let her go like you ordered us to," replied Smee.

"*Let her go?*"

"You called across the water and told us to release her."

"*I gave no such order!*" declared Hook, shaking with rage. "Something strange is going on here!"

The captain stood up and stared through the

"Why Don't We Kidnap the Boys' Mother?"

gloom at the water.

"Spirit that haunts this dark lagoon tonight, do you hear me?" he shouted.

Peter could never resist a game, and he answered in his imitation of Hook's voice, "Odds, bobs, hammer and tongs, I hear you!"

Smee and Starkey clung to each other in sheer terror.

"Who are you, stranger?" Hook shouted.

"I am James Hook, captain of the *Jolly Roger*."

"You are not! *I* am Captain Hook!"

"Brimstone and gall!" the voice answered. "Say that again, and I'll cast anchor in you!"

Hook tried a gentler approach.

"Ho," he called, "do you have another voice?"

"Yes," came the answer.

"Are you an animal?"

"No."

"Vegetable?"

"No."

In Sheer Terror

"Mineral?"

"No again."

"Are you a man?"

"No."

"A boy?"

"Yes."

"Just an ordinary boy?" puzzled Hook.

"No. You can't guess, can't guess!" Peter teased him. "Do you give up?"

"Yes," said the pirate wearily.

"Well then, I'll tell you. I am Peter Pan!"

In a moment, Hook recovered.

"Now we have him!" he leered at his men. "Into the water, Smee! Mind the boat, Starkey! Take him dead or alive!"

Hook leaped as he spoke. He could hear Peter's cheery voice floating across the water.

"Are you ready, boys?" Peter called out.

"Ay, ay!" came the replies from various parts of the lagoon.

The fight was short and fierce. First to draw

"Just an Ordinary Boy?"

blood was John, who climbed bravely onto the pirate ship, grabbed Starkey, and tore away his weapon. He wriggled overboard, and Starkey leaped after him. The boat drifted away. In another part of the lagoon, Smee plunged his corkscrew at Tootles but was himself bloodied by Curly.

Peter Pan and Captain Hook confronted each other on the rock. It wasn't planned that way, but they had scaled the rock from opposite sides, slid on the slippery surface, and, reaching out to grip something, found the other's arm.

Peter snatched a knife from Hook's belt and was about to drive it into the pirate's body when he realized that he was higher up on the rock than his enemy. It wouldn't have been a fair fight. He gave the pirate a hand to help him up.

Suddenly the iron hand clawed him. Hook clearly didn't share Peter's fondness for fair

The Fight Was Short and Fierce.

play!

All of a sudden, Hook broke away and began swimming wildly in the direction of the pirate ship.

The crocodile was in hot pursuit!

The Iron Hand Clawed Him.

They Sailed Through the Lagoon.

Chapter 9

The Kite and the Bird

The boys had lost both Peter and Wendy. They found the empty ship and sailed it home.

"Peter! Wendy!" they shouted as they sailed through the lagoon. Only the mocking voices of the mermaids answered them. As the boat left the lagoon behind, silence fell. Then came a feeble cry.

"Help! Help!"

Two small figures were leaning against the rock; the girl had fainted and lay on the boy's arm. With the last of his strength, Peter pulled

Wendy up to the rock and then lay down to catch his breath. He saw the water rising and that they would drown, but for the first time in his life he felt helpless.

A mermaid caught Wendy by the feet and began pulling her into the water. Peter managed to draw her back, but he told her the sad news.

"We are on the rock, but it is growing smaller. Soon the water will cover it."

"We must go," she said, still not fully understanding the terrible situation they faced. "Shall we swim home or fly?"

"Do you think you could swim or fly as far as the island, Wendy, without my help?"

She confessed that she was too tired. Peter moaned.

"What's wrong?" she asked, beginning to worry.

"I can't help you, Wendy. Hook clawed me. I can't swim or fly."

A Mermaid Caught Wendy's Feet.

"Do you mean we shall both drown?"

"Look how the water is rising!"

They covered their eyes to shut out the sight. Then they felt something brush against them. It was the tail of Michael's kite that had blown out of his hand and floated away. Peter seized the tail.

"The kite lifted Michael off the ground," he told Wendy. "Why couldn't it carry you?"

"Both of us!" she smiled.

"It can't lift two; Michael and Curly tried," he answered.

"Then let's draw lots!"

"Never! You are a lady. You must go!"

He tied the tail around her. She clung to him and refused to go without him, but Peter was firm.

"Goodbye, Wendy," he said as he pushed her toward the sky. In a few moments, she disappeared from sight, and Peter was alone on the rock. It was already so small that there was

"Goodbye, Wendy."

hardly room to stand.

"To die will be the biggest adventure of my life," he thought as he stared at the rising waters and listened to the mermaids calling to the moon. Soon they retired to their bed-chambers in coral caves under the lagoon.

The waters covered Peter's feet. Only a few inches more, and they would gobble up the boy entirely.

Something was moving on the lagoon. It looked like a piece of floating paper. Peter thought it must be part of the kite. He wondered what would happen first: would the paper drift to shore, or would he drown?

The thing was not a piece of paper. It was the Never bird, standing on her nest and fighting the tide to try to reach Peter. She spoke to him slowly and distinctly:

"I ... want ... you ... to ... get ... into ... the ... nest ... and ... then ... you ... can ... drift ... ashore, but ... I am ... too tired ... to bring

It Was the Never Bird.

it . . . any . . . nearer . . . so . . . you . . . must . . . try
to . . . swim . . . to it."

Peter was upset and forgot his manners.

"What are you quacking about?" he asked
rudely.

The bird repeated her message, and Peter
snapped at her again. Finally the bird lost her
temper. "You dumb head, why don't you do as
I tell you?"

"Shut up!" Peter retorted.

Nevertheless, the Never bird was deter-
mined to rescue him. With one last mighty effort, she pushed the nest against the rock.
Then she flew upward, abandoning her eggs,
so that he would comprehend her message.

Finally, Peter understood. He clutched the
nest and waved his tanks to the bird as she
fluttered overhead, waiting to see what he
would do with her two large white eggs.

Peter remembered that there was a stave on
the rock that some pirates had driven into it

The Bird Lost Her Temper.

to mark the site of buried treasure. The boys
had discovered the gold and jewels and liked
to toss them around for fun. Starkey had hung
his hat on the stave. It was deep and water-
tight and had a broad brim. Peter put the eggs
into the hat and floated it onto the lagoon.

The Never bird was much relieved that her
eggs were safe. Peter got into the nest, raised
the stave to make a mast, and hung up his
shirt for a sail. The bird fluttered down upon
the hat and once more sat upon her eggs. Then
Peter and the Never bird went their separate
ways.

Peter reached the underground house almost as soon as Wendy arrived by kite.

Peter Put the Eggs in the Hat.

The Indians Became His Friends.

Chapter 10

The Last Night on the Island

The Indians could not thank Peter enough for rescuing Tiger Lily, and they became his faithful friends and allies against the pirates. Peter liked to pretend that he was the Great Father and that the warriors were protecting his wigwam from the pirates.

Everyone knew that the pirates' attack would not be long in coming, but no one realized that this was to be the family's last night in the cozy underground house.

On this particular night, Peter went out to

get the time while the rest of the family ate a make-believe dinner. The way to get the time was to find the crocodile and stay near him until his clock struck.

No one really knew what day or night it was, of course. The Neverland was many moons away from England. But they pretended it was Saturday and had a lovely evening dancing and singing. Then Wendy told the children to get ready for bed, and when Peter returned they sat by the fire.

"I was just thinking," Peter confessed, looking a little frightened. "It's only make-believe, isn't it, that I am their father?"

"Of course!" Wendy answered.

"That's good," he said, "because it would make me seem so old to be their real father."

Wendy sighed. "You should be ashamed of yourself, Peter."

She tucked the children in bed, and now it was time for her story. Tonight she told the

Dancing and Singing

story that Peter hated most.

"There once was a gentleman..." she began.

"I had rather he had been a lady," Curly interrupted.

"Oh, mommy," cried Nibs, "there is a lady also, isn't there? She isn't dead, is she?"

"Oh, no!" Wendy reassured him. "There was a lady too. Their names were Mr. and Mrs. Darling."

"I knew them!" said John.

"I think I knew them too," chirped Michael.

"They had three children," Wendy continued. "And the children had a faithful nurse called Nana. But one night Mr. Darling got angry at Nana and chained her up in the yard, and so all the children flew away."

"Where did they go?" asked Tootles, who already knew the answer.

"They flew to the Neverland, where the lost children are," Wendy told them for the

"There Once Was..."

umpteenth time.

"Oh, Wendy!" cried Tootles, "was one of the lost children called Tootles?"

"Yes, he was."

"See, I'm in one of Wendy's stories!" Tootles announced to the other boys.

"Me too!" shouted Curly. "Wasn't one of the lost children called Curly?"

"Yes," said Wendy.

"How about the rest of us?" chimed in the twins.

"Yes, all of you," said Wendy. "Now be quiet and think about the feelings of the unhappy parents with all their children flown away."

"Ooh!" They moaned obediently, but they didn't really care.

"Think of the empty beds!" she said.

"I guess it *is* sad," Nibs conceded.

"I don't see how it can have a happy ending," said Slightly.

"If you knew how great is a mother's love,"

"I'm in One of Wendy's Stories!"

Wendy told them, "you would have no fear." She had now reached the part of the story that Peter hated most.

"I *do* like a mother's love," said Tootles, hitting Nibs with a pillow. "Do you like a mother's love, Nibs?"

"Yes, I do," said Nibs, hitting him back.

"You see," Wendy continued, "the children in the story knew that their mother would always leave the window open for them to fly back, so they stayed away for years and had a lovely time."

"Did they ever go back home?" asked the twins.

"Let us now peer into the future," said Wendy solemnly. "Many years have passed, and who is this beautiful lady getting off the train at London Station?"

"Oh, Wendy, who is she?" cried Nibs, every bit as excited as if he didn't know.

"Can it be...yes...no...it *is*...the fair

"Do You Like a Mother's Love?"

Wendy! And who are her two noble companions, now full-grown men? Can they be John and Michael? Yes, they are!"

"Oh!"

" 'See, dear brothers,' says Wendy, pointing upward, 'the window is still open. And now we are rewarded for our deep faith in a mother's love.' So up they flew to their mommy and daddy; and it's impossible to describe how happy the reunion was!"

When Wendy finished the story, Peter let out a deep groan.

They all rushed to his side to try to calm him down. Then he told them something that he had never revealed to anyone:

"Long ago," he began, "I thought as you do that my mother would always keep the window open for me, so I stayed away for many moons and then flew back. But the window was locked, because my mother had forgotten all about me and there was another little boy

Something He Had Never Revealed

sleeping in my bed."

It's hard to know whether this was true, but Peter thought it was true and that was all that mattered.

"Are you sure that all mothers are like that?" Curly asked him.

"Yes, I'm sure."

But John and Michael weren't so sure.

"Let's go home, Wendy!" they cried.

"Yes!" she said, hugging them.

"Not tonight!" wailed the lost boys.

"Yes, we must go at once!" Wendy declared. "Our mother may already be mourning us as dead!"

She turned to Peter. "Will you make the necessary arrangements for our journey?"

"If you wish," he replied, trying to stay calm. But he actually minded very much and was full of anger at grown-ups, who always spoiled everything.

He gave instructions to the Indians and

"Let's Go Home, Wendy!"

then got inside his tree and took lots of quick breaths.

Peter returned to the underground house to find a scene of panic. Terrified at the thought of losing Wendy, the lost boys had surrounded her angrily.

"We won't let her go!" said Nibs.

"Let's keep her prisoner!" declared Slightly.

"Ay, chain her up!" shouted the twins.

Wendy appealed to Tootles.

"I am just Tootles," he responded, "and nobody minds me. But I will draw the blood of anybody who doesn't treat Wendy like a lady!"

Peter made his opinion plain: He would not hold Wendy in the Neverland against her will.

"I have asked the Indians to guide you through the woods, since flying makes you so tired. Then Tinker Bell will take you across the sea."

"Thank you, Peter."

"Wake up, Tink!" called Peter. The fairy was

A Scene of Panic

not sleeping. She was listening to the conversation and, although she was glad to see Wendy depart, she didn't wish to be her escort.

"Don't bother me!" she shrieked.

Peter wasn't used to such disobedience.

"Get dressed at once, Tink, or I will open your curtains, and all the boys will see you in your nightgown!"

The fairy was ready in an instant.

Wendy turned to the lost boys. Looking at their sad faces, she felt a surge of pity for them.

"Dear children," she said, "If you will all come with me, I am almost sure that my mother and father will adopt you!"

The invitation was meant especially for Peter, but the other boys jumped for joy.

"Won't they think we're a handful?" Nibs asked in the middle of his jump.

"Oh, no!" Wendy reassured them. "We'll just put a few beds in the living-room."

"Don't Bother Me!"

"Can we go, Peter?" they asked.

"All right," he replied, with bitterness in his voice. And they raced to get their things ready.

"And now, Peter, let me give you some medicine before you go," said Wendy, thinking that he would join them. Of course, it was only water that she gave him, but she counted the drops carefully to make it seem more like a dose of medicine.

When she was finished, Peter declared, "I'm not going with you, Wendy."

"You must come, Peter!" she coaxed.

"No!"

"But you must find your mother!"

"No, I wouldn't want to find her! She might say I was getting old, and I just always want to be a little boy and to have fun."

There was nothing left for Wendy to do but to tell the boys that Peter wasn't coming. They stared at him in disbelief, but they knew they couldn't change his mind.

They Raced to Get Their Things Ready.

"If you find your mothers," he declared sternly, "I hope you will like them."

Then he turned to Wendy and held out his hand.

"Goodbye," he said simply.

"Will you remember to change your clothes regularly, Peter?" she asked.

"Yes, of course."

"And to take your medicine?"

"Yes."

Peter showed no emotion.

"Are you ready, Tinker Bell?" he called out.

"Ay, ay," the fairy replied.

"Then lead the way!"

"Goodbye," He Said Simply.

Peter Grabbed His Sword.

Chapter 11

The Kidnapping

Tink darted up the nearest tree, but no one followed her, because at this very moment the pirates launched their horrible attack against the Indians. The stillness of the night was broken by screams and the clash of steel. In the house underground, Wendy and the boys looked at Peter, wondering what he would do. Without saying a word, he grabbed his sword.

The Indians could have assembled a fighting force if they had moved quickly, but their tribal rules stated that it is not permitted to display surprise in the presence of enemies. Thus, when the pirates suddenly appeared, the Indians remained still for a moment too long before they picked up their weapons.

The Indians fought valiantly and took many pirates down to the death with them. But sadly the final outcome was a complete massacre of the Indians.

And still the work of the pirates was not done. Destroying the Indians was only the first part of their task. The main goal was to kill Peter Pan and his band—but especially Peter himself!

It is hard to imagine that a big strong man like Hook was so obsessed with a small boy. Peter, of course, had fed Hook's arm to the crocodile; but Hook was bothered even more by Peter's personality. The boy was such a show-off! Hook couldn't wait to strike him down forever!

But how were the pirates to get down

The Indians Fought Valiantly.

through the trees to the underground house?

Down below, Peter's "family" remained silent. They stared at each other with frightened expressions. They knew from the stillness above that the battle was over, but how could they find out who had won?

"If the Indians have won," Peter said at last, "they will beat the tom-tom. That is always their sign of victory."

The pirates, listening to the conversation below, grinned wickedly. Hook motioned to Smee to beat the tom-tom. After two beats, he heard Peter cry joyfully:

"The tom-tom! The Indians are victorious!"

The children, not realizing what doom awaited them, let out a mighty cheer, after which they repeated their goodbyes to Peter. The farewells puzzled the pirates but were soon forgotten as they waited eagerly for their enemies to come up the trees. Hook ordered one man to each tree and told the remaining

But Who Had Won?

members of the band to stand by.

First to emerge was Curly, who fell into the waiting arms of the pirate Cecco and was passed, like a bale of hay, from one man to another until he fell at the feet of Hook himself. All the boys were plucked from their trees in the same manner.

Wendy came last and received a different treatment. Hook, an unlikely gentleman, tipped his hat to her, offered her his arm, and escorted her to the spot where the others were being gagged. She was too surprised to cry out; after all, Wendy was just a little girl.

The pirates tied up the children with ropes to prevent them from flying away. They doubled them up, with their knees close to their ears. The poor boys looked like turkeys about to be put in the oven for roasting!

Everything went according to Hook's plan until Slightly's turn came. The pirates wrapped the ropes around him, but there

Hook Offered Her His Arm.

wasn't a long enough piece of rope left to tie a knot. Three times they tried. Then they poked around his body to find the cause of the problem. What they found surprised and delighted Hook.

Slightly drank huge amounts of water, which caused him to swell far beyond the size of the other boys. Instead of reducing his weight so that he could fit into the passageway of his tree, he had increased the size of the passageway to accommodate his body. He had never told the other boys about this, but now Hook knew his secret! The wicked pirate would soon use this priceless information to descend into the underground house and try to kill Peter.

Hook ordered his men to carry the children to the pirate ship. He also thought up a clever way to transport them. The children were tossed into Wendy's little house, which was borne on the shoulders of the pirates. Hook

Not Enough Rope to Tie a Knot

stayed behind on the island.

When night fell, the evil Captain Hook tiptoed to Slightly's tree. He slipped out of his black cloak and stepped into the hole that Slightly had whittled in the trunk. Then, struggling to overcome his fear of the unknown, he let himself slide down the passageway.

He landed safely at the bottom and looked around with great curiosity. It didn't take long to find Peter—the boy was fast asleep on the huge bed.

A feeling of rage came over Hook. He lurched toward the sleeping boy but tripped over the door of Slightly's tree. It didn't completely fill the opening, and he had been looking over it toward Peter. Hook reached for the latch, but it was too low for him to reach. Was Peter to escape Hook's fury after all?

Suddenly the captain caught sight of Peter's medicine standing on a ledge within easy

Hook Tiptoed to Slightly's Tree.

reach. The pirate always carried a poisonous drug that he could swallow if an enemy ever captured him alive. He added five drops of this dreadful yellow liquid to the medicine in Peter's cup.

Then, throwing a final glance at the sleeping boy, he stole up the tree and emerged into the night. He donned his cloak and hat and walked rapidly through the woods.

A Poisonous Drug

Peter Reached for His Dagger.

Chapter 12

A Close Call For Peter

Peter slept soundly the whole night. It was 10:00 in the morning by the crocodile's clock when he finally awoke. A tapping on the door of his tree broke the stillness of the morning. Peter reached for his dagger.

"Who's there?"

No one answered.

"I won't open the door unless you speak," he said.

At last, he heard a bell-like voice from the other side.

"Let me in, Peter."

Tinker Bell flew in, flushed with excitement. Her dress was stained with mud.

"What's wrong, Tink?"

"Wendy and the boys have been captured!"

She described how they had been taken to the pirate ship and bound.

"I'll rescue them!" cried Peter, leaping for his weapons. He also wanted to do something to please Wendy. He picked up the cup with his medicine.

"No!" shrieked Tink, who had heard Hook muttering about his evil deed as he sped through the woods toward the ship.

"Why shouldn't I take my medicine?" asked Peter with a puzzled look on his face.

"It is poisoned!"

"Poisoned? Who could have poisoned it?"

"Hook."

"Don't be silly! How could Hook have gotten down here?"

Tinker Bell Flew in.

Alas, Tinker Bell could not explain, for she didn't know the secret of Slightly's tree. But Hook's muttering had left no room for doubt.

As Peter raised the cup to his mouth, Tink flew between his lips and the container and drained it to the last drop.

"How dare you drink my medicine?" Peter challenged her.

The fairy didn't answer. Already she was reeling in the air.

"What's the matter with you?" he asked in an anxious voice.

"It was poisoned, and now I'm going to die," she said softly.

"Oh, Tink, did you drink it to save me?"

"Yes," she replied, tottering toward her chamber. She collapsed onto her bed. Every moment, her light grew paler; if it went out, she would be dead.

Peter leaned close to her as she tried to whisper something. She was saying that she

Tink Drained It to the Last Drop.

thought she could recover if children still believed in fairies.

There were no longer any children in the house, but Peter appealed to all of those who might be dreaming of the Neverland.

"Do you believe?" he cried out to them.

Tink sat up in bed to catch the voices that would decide her fate. She thought she heard many say "yes."

"If you believe, clap your hands! Don't let Tink die!" Peter begged.

Many clapped, but some didn't. Then all the clapping stopped, as if mothers all around the world had rushed to their nurseries to see what was happening.

But already Tink was saved. Her voice grew stronger. She began to flash merrily through the room.

"And now to rescue Wendy!" said Peter.

He sprinted from his tree, holding his weapons tightly. He wanted to fly, but his

"Do You Believe?" He Cried Out.

shadow would have been reflected in the light of the moon and alerted his enemies to his presence. So he plodded, Indian fashion, through the forest. Not a single living thing except the crocodile passed him, and the air was deathly silent.

Peter swore a terrible oath: "It's Hook or me this time!"

"It's Hook or Me!"

Peter Approached the Pirate Ship.

Chapter 13

The Pirate Ship

Jolly Roger was an odd name for a ship that was far from being a happy place. Some of the most wicked and bloody deeds in pirate history had been plotted and carried out on this vessel.

As Peter approached the pirate ship, he saw only a single greenish light marking the spot where it lay at anchor near the mouth of the lagoon. A few of the pirates, shouting heavily and laughing, were leaning over the edge of the ship. Another group was busy gambling.

Still others, exhausted from the hard work of carrying the house full of boys, were sprawled on the deck, asleep.

Captain Hook paced back and forth, sometimes stumbling against one of the sleeping mates. He was lost in thought. This should have been his hour of triumph. He had gotten rid of Peter Pan (or so he believed), and all the other boys were on the ship and would soon be forced to walk the plank.

Nevertheless, Hook was very sad because he felt so terribly alone. The men in his band were of a much lower class than he. He was very aware of his superior position and breeding. He regarded his shipmates as not much better than the beasts on the island.

The drunken pirates were dancing wildly around the ship now. Hook scolded them, reminding them that there was important business to conduct.

"Are all the children chained, so that they

Hook Paced Back and Forth.

can't fly away?" he asked.

"Ay, ay!"

"Then hoist them up!"

The prisoners were hauled out—all except Wendy—and placed in a line in front of Hook.

"Now then, bullies," the captain grinned, "six of you will walk the plank tonight, but I need two cabin boys. Which of you wants to sign up?"

Tootles stepped forward, dragging his chains. He looked solemnly at the captain.

"You see, sir, I don't think my mother would like me to be a pirate. Would your mother want you to be a pirate, Slightly?"

"I don't think so," the boy replied. "How about you, Nibs? What would your mother say?"

"She would agree with yours. Curly, what would . . ."

"Shut up, all of you!" interrupted Hook. He turned to John.

"You, boy, have you ever thought about being

The Prisoners Were Hauled Out.

a pirate?"

John, who had followed the conversation in silence, seemed pleased that the captain had chosen him.

"I might want to be a pirate. I once thought of calling myself Red-handed Jack," he confessed.

"That's a good name!" grinned Hook. "That's exactly what we'll call you if you join us!"

"What would you call *me* if *I* join?" Michael called out.

"Blackbeard Joe."

"What do you think, John?" Michael asked his brother.

"What do *you* think?" John replied.

"You have to decide. You're older!"

John turned to Hook.

"Would we still be respectful subjects of the king of England?" he asked in a very serious manner.

Anger flashed across the captain's face.

"I Might Want to Be a Pirate."

"Absolutely not! You would have to swear, 'Down with the king,'" he replied.

"Then I refuse to become a pirate!" snapped John.

"I refuse too!" echoed Michael.

Hook was furious.

"That seals your doom!" he roared. "Bring up their mother and get the plank ready!" he ordered.

No words can describe Wendy's intense hatred for the pirates. The boys might have been attracted by the adventures of piracy; but Wendy, who was very fussy around her surroundings, noticed only that the pirate ship was filthy. She was willing to bet that no one had ever scrubbed it! The dirt and garbage were disgusting to a girl of her fine upbringing.

The glass on the ship's portholes was so full of grease that Wendy was able to write on it with her finger. She did so, scrawling the words "Dirty Pig" on every little window.

"I Refuse Too!"

"So, my beautiful lady, you will see your children walk the plank," said Hook, eyeing her with a wicked grin as she was brought to the deck.

"Will they die?" inquired Wendy in a voice full of scorn.

"Yes!" he snarled. "Hush, everyone! It's time for a mother's last words to her children."

Wendy did not hesitate, and her performance was awesome.

"These are my final words, dear boys," she said, gazing from one to the other fondly. "I believe that I have a message to you from your real mothers, and it is this: 'We hope that our sons will die like English gentlemen.'"

The pirates, deeply impressed, were silent; but the boys cried out passionately.

"I will do what my mother hopes!" Tootles swore. "What will you do, Nibs?"

"What my mother hopes! How about you, Slightly?"

"See Your Children Walk the Plank."

"What my mother hopes. Curly, what are..."

"Enough!" roared Hook. "Tie her up, Smee!"

As he bound Wendy to the mast, Smee whispered, "I'll save you, honey, if you promise to be my mother!"

Wendy looked away in disgust.

"I would almost rather have no children at all," she replied, realizing that even if she agreed to his promise she could not rescue the boys.

The eyes of all the children were fastened to the plank. They wanted to die like men, but their courage melted away and they stood shivering in fright.

Hook moved toward Wendy, intending to turn her face toward the plank so that she would see each boy take his final walk. But he never reached her, because at that moment he heard the terrible tick-tick of the crocodile!

An unbelievable change came over the cap-

He Bound Wendy to the Mast.

tain. He was transformed from a fearsome monster to a pitiful creature looking for a place to hide. A terrifying thought pierced his brain: "The crocodile is about to board the ship!"

The boys, dragging their chains with them, moved to the edge of the ship to watch the animal's approach. But, wondrous to tell, there was no crocodile. Instead, they saw Peter Pan!

Signaling the boys to remain silent so as not to arouse the pirates' suspicion, Peter continued to imitate the ticking sound of the crocodile.

Looking for a Place to Hide

The Crocodile Wasn't Ticking.

Chapter 14

"Hook Or Me!"

Thunderstruck at Tinker Bell's news that the pirates had kidnapped Wendy and the children, Peter had not wasted a moment. He scampered across the island, one hand gripping his dagger tightly.

On the way to the lagoon, he saw the crocodile and noticed that it wasn't ticking. He realized at once that the clock had stopped working. Since Peter—as the reader knows— could imitate anything, he began to make the ticking noise so that the beasts on the island would think he was the crocodile and so let him pass without attacking him. When he reached the water and started to swim, he just kept on ticking.

Peter was a very fast swimmer, and he reached the ship in seconds. He climbed aboard without making a sound—or so he believed. He was greatly surprised, therefore, to see the pirates huddled together in one corner of the deck around Hook, who looked as frightened as if he had just heard the crocodile.

The crocodile! Peter looked around quickly, expecting to catch a glimpse of the animal. Then he remembered that he himself was making the tick-tick sound.

At that moment, Ed Teynte, the quartermaster, came out of the ship's cabin and approached the spot where Peter Pan was standing. Peter had wonderfully quick reflexes, and he plunged his dagger deep into the pirate's body.

Peter Reached the Ship in Seconds.

John, standing nearby, covered the victim's mouth to muffle his dying scream. The pirate staggered forward. Four of the boys caught him so that he wouldn't fall to the deck and make a loud thud. Peter motioned to them to throw the body overboard. There was a splash and then silence. The entire operation took only a few short minutes.

Peter tiptoed into the cabin. The pirates remained huddled together, expecting the crocodile to pounce momentarily upon their captain; but as soon as the dreaded ticking sound disappeared, they began to relax.

Hook recovered his courage and returned his attention to the prisoners. He hated the boys more than ever because they had seen him appear weak and cowardly when he thought the crocodile was coming.

"Do you want a touch of the cat before you walk the plank?" Hook asked the children.

"No!" they cried in a single voice, falling to

A Splash and then Silence

their knees for mercy.

Hook grinned wickedly. "Fetch the cat, Jukes!" he ordered. "It's in the cabin."

The cabin! Peter was in the cabin! The boys stared at each other.

Suddenly an eerie scream pierced the air, hovered over the ship, and then died away.

It was followed by a peculiar crowing sound—a sound that mystified the pirates but that the boys recognized instantly as Peter's crow of victory.

"What on earth was that?" roared Hook.

Cecco ran into the cabin. He returned with a look of horror.

"Jukes is dead!" he announced. "Someone stabbed him! And the cabin is as black as midnight!"

"Cecco, go back and fetch me the murderer!" the captain ordered.

Cecco was the bravest of all Hook's men, but this time he hesitated. Hook raised his iron

"Fetch the Cat!"

claw, forcing Cecco to obey. Again the deathly screech was heard, followed by Peter's crow.

"Enough!" thundered Hook. "Who will go to the cabin and bring the killer out?" His gaze fixed on Starkey.

"Didn't I hear you volunteer?" Hook asked, with a sly grin.

"No, by thunder!" the terrified mate cried.

"But I believe you did!" insisted the captain, raising his iron claw in a threatening gesture.

"Let's wait until Cecco returns," Starkey pleaded. The rest of the crew nodded in support.

"I would advise you to volunteer immediately!" growled Hook, bringing the claw directly over Starkey's head.

"I'd rather hang!" Starkey declared.

"Is this a mutiny?" asked Hook sharply.

"Captain, have mercy!" Starkey whimpered.

Hook brought the claw down to within inches of Starkey's skull. None of the other pirates

"Who Will Bring the Killer Out?"

dared to interfere.

With a scream of despair, the doomed man threw himself upon Long Tom and leaped overboard.

Everyone was silent for a moment. Then the captain cursed the remaining crew members.

"Do any of you other gentlemen wish to start a mutiny?" asked Hook in a steely voice.

There was no reply.

"You're all cowards!" he sneered. "I'll fetch the killer myself!"

Seizing a lantern and shaking his iron claw, the captain strode briskly to the cabin. A moment later, he returned without the lantern.

"Something blew out the light," he explained weakly.

"What happened to Cecco?" the other pirates asked.

"He's as dead as Jukes!" replied Hook.

The captain's reluctance to re-enter the cabin made a poor impression on his band.

Starkey Threw Himself on Long Tom.

Hints of mutiny arose again.

"The ship is doomed!" cried one mate.

The children could not help cheering. Hook, quarreling with his men, had almost forgotten about the prisoners.

"Here's an idea, bullies!" he said to the crew. "Open the door and drive the children in. Let them fight the murderer! If they kill him, so much the better; if he kills them, we're none the worse!"

The boys pretended to struggle as they were pushed into the cabin and the door was closed behind them. Wendy, still tied to the ship's mast, waited eagerly for Peter to reappear.

Peter had found what he was searching for in the cabin: the key to unlock the children's chains. He wasted no time in freeing them. Then he and the boys opened the door and crept forward onto the deck, armed with whatever weapons they had discovered. Motioning for them to hide, Peter cut the ropes binding

The Children Could Not Help Cheering.

Wendy.

Peter and his companions were now free to fly away together, but something held him back.

It was his oath: "Hook or me this time!"

Peter told Wendy to hide with the boys. He took her place at the mast and wrapped her cloak around him so that he would be mistaken for her. Then he took a big breath and let out the same cry that he had made after killing the pirates in the cabin.

Hearing the cry, Hook's remaining men fell into a panic. They turned to attack the captain.

"Wait!" shouted Hook. "No pirate ship ever had any luck with a woman on board. Toss the girl into the sea!"

The crew members rushed toward the figure in the cloak, who had stood as still as a statue so that they would think she was still bound.

"Nobody can save you now, missy!" one of the pirates jeered.

He Took Her Place at the Mast.

"There *is* somebody!" the figure answered.

"Who may that be?"

"It's Peter Pan, come to seek revenge!" he shouted, flinging off the cloak and revealing his real identity.

At that moment, Hook's willpower collapsed.

"Down, boys, and at them!" Peter yelled.

A loud clanging of weapons and shouts of glee resounded on the ship as the boys took their revenge on the pirate band. The pirates might have won if they had stuck together; but, instead, they ran here and there, striking wildly and each man thinking only of his personal survival.

Finally, all the pirates except Hook were dead. But he, even alone, seemed a match for the entire group. Repeatedly, they closed in on him, and repeatedly he cleared a new space for himself.

"Put away your swords, boys!" a loud voice rang out. "This man belongs to me!"

"There *Is* Somebody!"

Thus, Hook found himself face to face with Peter Pan.

"Dark and evil man, I will have you!" Peter shouted.

The deciding contest began. Hook held a great advantage because of his massive size and weight, but Peter fluttered around so rapidly that he always managed to escape the enemy's blade.

Even the dreaded iron claw was unable to save the captain. Finally, watching Peter slowly move toward him through the air with his dagger ready to strike the fatal blow, Hook sprang upon the ship's mast and leaped into the sea. There, unknown to him, the crocodile lay silently waiting.

Thus perished Captain James Hook, one of the most famous and feared pirates in history!

Face to Face

Peter Became the Captain.

Chapter 15

The Return Home

The victors sailed the ship toward the mainland. Peter, of course, became the captain. He sat proudly in the cabin with Hook's feathered hat on his head and one hand held threateningly in the air like a claw. He wore an outfit that Wendy had sewn from pieces of Hook's clothes.

Peter studied the ship's maps and decided that they could reach the Azores Islands by June 21st, after which they could get home faster by flying.

One fateful Thursday, Mrs. Darling was asleep in her chair in the nursery when

Wendy, John and Michael flew in through the open window and landed quietly on the floor.

"I think I have been here before," ventured Michael.

"Of course you have!" Wendy smiled. "There is your bed!"

"And there is the kennel!" exclaimed John, rushing over to peer inside.

"Nana's not here!" he announced. "There's a man inside!"

The children gathered around.

"It's Father!" said Wendy, startled.

"But he's not even as big as the pirate that I killed!" sighed Michael.

"And there's Mother, sitting in her chair!" Wendy cried.

"Then you are not really our mother!" Michael scolded his sister.

"Let's all get into our beds so she can find us there!" Wendy suggested.

Mrs. Darling did indeed find them, but in

They Landed Quietly on the Floor.

her dreams she had seen them in their beds so many times that she believed herself to be dreaming again. She returned to her chair and sat down. The children were terribly upset, and tears welled up in their eyes.

"Mother!" Wendy cried.

"That's Wendy!" said Mrs. Darling, still not sure if it was a dream.

"Mother!"

"That's John!"

"Mother!" Michael chimed in.

Together, they ran to her and, as if in a daze, she wrapped her arms around them.

"George!" she cried out when she found her voice. "Come quickly!"

He emerged from the kennel and embraced the children. Nana ran in to share the great joy.

Peter Pan, watching the happy scene from outside the window, wondered sadly whether any of the exciting adventures he experienced could compare with this beautiful family scene.

"That's Wendy!"

The Boys Waited Patiently Downstairs.

Chapter 16

Forgetting How To Fly

The other boys waited patiently downstairs to give Wendy time to tell her parents about them. When they entered the room, they stood in a row in front of the Darlings, took off their hats, and looked shamefully at their pirate clothes.

Mrs. Darling agreed to let them stay, but Mr. Darling wondered how the family budget would support six extra children. Mrs. Darling was ashamed of her husband's behavior, and he finally agreed to find space in the living room for them.

Peter, still hovering outside the window, said a final goodbye to Wendy. Mrs. Darling stood beside her daughter, still fearful that she might disappear once again. She told Peter that she would adopt all the other boys and would like to have him too.

"Would you send me to school?" he asked suspiciously.

"Yes."

"And then to an office?"

"I suppose so."

"Would I soon become a man?"

"Very soon."

Peter shuddered.

"I don't want to do those things!" he said. "No one is going to catch me and make me a grown up!"

"But where will you live?" Mrs. Darling wondered.

"With Tinker Bell in the house that we built

"Would You Send Me to School?"

for Wendy," he replied. "The fairies will put the house high up in the tree tops where they sleep at night."

"How lovely!" Wendy exclaimed in a tone of such wistfulness that her mother gripped her hand to make sure she didn't fly off with Peter at that very moment.

"I thought all the fairies were dead," Mrs. Darling remarked.

"There are always a lot of new ones," Wendy explained patiently. She repeated to her mother what Peter had taught her on this subject: "When a new baby laughs for the first time, a new fairy is born. And since there are always new babies, there are always new fairies. They live in nests on the tops of trees. The purple ones are boys and the white ones are girls."

"Will you come with me to the little house, Wendy?" asked Peter hopefully.

"May I, please, mommy?"

"Certainly not!" declared Mrs. Darling.

Her Mother Gripped Her Hand.

"Now that you're home again, I plan to keep you here!"

"But Peter really needs a mother!" she protested.

"So do you, my lovely daughter!" replied Mrs. Darling.

Finally, Peter flew away, but not before receiving a promise from Wendy and her mother that she could come with him once a year to the Neverland for spring cleaning.

So every year, until she became quite grown up, Wendy went to the Neverland. In time, Wendy married and was truly a mother. And then her daughter Jane flew to the Neverland with Peter.

Then it was Margaret's turn, Jane's daughter. Someday Margaret's daughter will get to fly to the Neverland. And so it will go on forever and ever, as long as children believe in their dreams.